FIRST KISS

BY
EIRA JACOB

TABLE OF CONTENTS

CHAPTER ONE

A high school classmate of mine recently returned from our high school reunion. She had not attended one in a few years; we stayed in touch off and on but have never gone back to my old high school town.

She emailed me a group picture of three dozen or so of our classmates. I was fascinated; while a few were easily recognizable, many were not. She helped me put names with the faces in the picture. Many had dramatically changed in appearance over the years; most had put on a little too much weight and all of the men were either balding or very gray. Among the women it was somewhat of a mixed bag. Two or three were quite attractive in their late fifties, even having become more so with age.

There was one girl not in the picture. She left for college within days of graduation. She never returned nor did she stay in touch. Her parents left the area soon after she graduated. Everyone remembers liking her; she had no enemies, far from it. She was voted "nicest" and "most friendly". She was never part of a clique; she was liked and respected in every high school social circle. Many of us have tried to track her down but she seems to have vanished.

She was taller than her peers; I always sensed that she was sensitive about her height and slumped her shoulders so as not to appear taller than her classmates. She had problems with her eyes. She wore very thick glasses.

She was shy and soft spoken; I don't remember her having a date for the senior prom. Boys didn't pursue or flirt with her. She was not on the list of the top, hot, "cute" high school date prospects. She had soft, straw colored hair cut short, a very light complexion, skin that would freckle in the sun and blue eyes. The dresses she wore were plain and loose fitting, giving no hint of her possible curves. She never wore a hint of makeup.

While she did not fit the profile of what guys saw as, "sexy" back then, no one viewed her as ugly or unattractive. If one of us had asked her to the senior prom, I believe that it would have met with approval from the other guys. "Great! You asked Elena to the prom. She's the nicest girl in our class." But, none of us did.

Looking through my high school yearbook; I lingered over her picture. She had removed her glasses for her senior photo; she seldom did so since she was blind without them. I wondered how I missed it forty years ago; she was a very pretty girl.

Let's assume that one of us did ask her to the prom and she accepted and started the story there.

That evening, corsage in hand, a young man went to her parent's door to pick her up and there was that flash of a Cinderella moment. Thanks to the radical new contact lens that she had just had fitted, she was not blind without her glasses but still forced to view the world through a blurry haze. The home made dress which she and her mother had made together was not sexy or revealing but was quite glamorous on her tall frame. And for the first time in too long she decided that her date was just tall enough for her to stand up straight.

Why had she made that decision? The boy who had asked her to the prom, a boy who could have had any girl in school, had always been kind and sweet to her since they had first met in fifth grade. He had been the one who had said, "dammit, Elena, you're a pretty girl stand up straight." He had been the first boy who had ever told her she was pretty. He had never flirted but nor had he ever ignored her. He had for as long as she could remember always said hello, and smiled when others were too busy in their own social world to see her. He had never before asked her out on a date. As strict as her parents were, she hadn't ever gone on a real date.

On that very special night Elena felt pretty. As she walked into the school gym on the arm of a devilishly handsome young man, she felt special. Heads turned as the couple entered; some didn't recognize the girl in the long, elegant white gown.

For Elena that evening was amazing, magical and memorable. Dustin a wonderful dancer and an attentive partner treated her like a princess and she felt like royalty. Boys who had never given her a second look asked her to dance but it was in Dustin's arms she felt completely safe and very much like Cinderella.

He had taken her home before the affair had ended. Her parents did not want her out past 1:00 AM. And on her front steps he had kissed her; it was the first real kiss she had ever experienced. He held her tightly in his arms and kissed her several times.

"Elena, you were the most beautiful girl at the prom. I was the envy of every other guy. Thank you for a very special night; I'll cherish it for the rest of my life. I wish...we made a pretty neat couple, don't you think? I'm a lucky guy to have been your friend all of these years."

Then he was gone. They saw each
other off and on during the remaining two
weeks of school. They hugged each other at
graduation, kissed with her parents standing
only a few feet away. Three days after
graduation she was off to summer school at
the state university. Her severe vision defect
had caused her problems on the SATs. Her
inability to read the small print had
heightened her anxiety and she had not
done well. Her high school record was
excellent and her teachers made strong
recommendations. She was admitted on a
probationary basis to summer school. If she
did well, she was in for the fall.

•••••••

When Elena got to the massive college
campus she had new glasses. Coupled with
her new contact lenses she had a clear view
of the printed page for the first time in her
life. She was neither stupid nor dumb; she
was gifted. Her vision, unrecognized in
those days, had held her back. Today,
special accommodations would be available;

back then it was, "tough luck, kid". She earned straight A's in the four classes she took during those two summer terms.

It was in the gap between summer classes and the fall term that providence struck. Her parents had moved far away. The money for a trip home for two weeks wasn't available. What was available at the university's medical school was a doctor who had perfected a radically new surgical procedure which could correct her vision. It would cost her nothing. By the time fall classes began, Elena had retired both her glasses and her contact lens. She could see perfectly for the first time in her life.

Elena had also vowed never to slump again. It was easier on the huge campus of over 30,000 students. She held several jobs throughout her college years. She had even modeled at a local department store where she got a significant discount. Her wardrobe became less homemade and more fashionable. Elena would never be busty but the little bumps on her chest grew to a respectable B.

She was an exceptional student; her professors took note and many invited her to their homes and became good friends. Her self confidence bloom and she became more self assured. She took electives in the speech and drama department and left the stage wowing the audience.

One warm spring's day when shorts were appropriate the long legged natural blond with the quick, friendly smile and the sparkling blue eyes turned many heads as she purposefully strode from one building to another.

Boys noticed her. Boys asked her out. A boy introduced her to alcohol and had sex with her. She cried herself to sleep over the night which followed. Embarrassed, ashamed, humiliated and scared, she vowed that it would never happen again, at least not that way.

She enjoyed other lovers during her undergraduate years; she had a brief affair with an older professor. She graduated, Summa Cum Laude and was accepted at an Ivy League Law school in one of the first classes to admit women. At a few weeks past her twenty-first birthday she was a stunning young woman. She was brilliant. She was confident and self assured but always friendly and caring. Sexually, she was mature; she knew what she liked and didn't like and was choosy.

The environment for female law students at the time was hostile; she endured demeaning and sexually harassing behavior from classmates and faculty alike. She graduated three years later, Juris Doctorate, second in her class and editor of Law Review. She accepted a clerkship with an Associate Justice of the Supreme Court of law in the United States.

CHAPTER TWO

Elena had become the beautiful Cinderella and the dreaded midnight hour was way in the past. She often thought about that magic evening with that special friend, that handsome boy who had given her that first kiss and wondered where he was and what he was doing with his life.

She had called her best friend from high school who had stayed in touch with the happenings in that small high school town. No one was sure what had happened to Dustin. He had taken a job about fifty miles away immediately following graduation. He had been slated to attend a respected University somewhere in the South Virginia, Georgia or one of the Carolinas. Someone thought he had gone into the military; the draft was still in effect and there was a war on.

Completing her clerkship, she took a job as an assistant federal prosecutor. The top private law firms still weren't hiring female attorneys with any prospect of making partner. A stint as a government lawyer could help her get noticed. Three years later she had excelled; by all rights she expected to be nominated within the year as a fully fledged Federal prosecutor.

While sexism still dominated the private arena, female attorneys had a leg up in the public sector and her record was impeccable. Many of her colleagues thought that she might just become a federal court judge by the time she was forty. Politics was politics and administrations change; a man with dramatically less impressive qualifications got the job.

Fortunately, she had been noticed; a top private firm, specializing in appeals work and reputed to have a strong commitment to developing female partners came courting. Within two years she was pleading cases in front of the Appeals Courts and winning them. Weeks before her thirtieth birthday, she became a full partner in one of the top law firms in the country specializing in constitutional law.

Every one of the nine Justices of the Supreme Court knew her by name. She was making more money in a year than her father had made in his whole life. She had no siblings. Her parents had her late in life and had been very strict. She knew they loved her in their own unique way but her relationship with them had been distant. It had become more so as the years had passed. She had enjoyed several reasonably meaningful relationships; she had come close to marriage but it had just not worked out. She owned more house than she needed with an acre of land on the edge of the District, sharing it with a pair of German Short Haired Pointers. She was between lovers and not seriously dating anyone. She was a success; she had made something of her life. Her always cheerful countenance toward others hid the loneliness that often haunted her. She wasn't an unhappy person but still there was an emptiness inside that she struggled to deal with.

As a full partner her hours would become more reasonable. She would have free time for the first time since she could remember. It scared her to death. Perhaps because of her fear and loneliness she entered into a relationship with a partner in the firm more than a decade her senior. He was attentive, caring and a competent lover.

It was not until she had accepted his proposal of marriage and become Mrs. Adams that they both realized that their marriage had been rash and ill advised. They quietly divorced a year later with no hatred and remained friends. Others in the firm marveled at how well the two dealt with each other following the divorce. They were two very nice people who, having mutually recognized their mistake, chose not to compound it with bad blood. They had been friends and continued to be friends and that was that.

One Friday afternoon Elena former husband, the firm's managing partner, graced her office doorway. "Got a second, E.A?" He said, using the initials that had become her official moniker within the office and in legal circles in general."Sure, Ben. I'm just taking one last look at a brief that I'm presenting Monday to the 5th.

What can I do for you?```"With Roy's stroke, I'm trying to ensure that his key clients are suitably distributed to the partners. I know you have a full plate but I don't think this one is going to take up much of your time."The Roy in question, Roy Roberts, had been one of the two founding partners of the firm. Elena had a very special place in her heart for the older gentleman.

He had fought for her to be hired, fought for her elevation to partner, mentored her and thrown cases her way that had been instrumental in building her legal reputation. She dearly loved the man old enough to be her grandfather; he was now in a hospital bed. The prognosis for recovery was dim. He would likely linger in a near comatose state for some time and ultimately expire within a year or less."Anything I can do to help." Elena replied.

"This one is one of Roy's personal clients. I'm pretty sure that he is the only one in the firm who has ever met the guy. Roy handled a copy write infringement case for him almost a decade ago which he won but since then any work the firm has done for him has been pretty mundane. Not a lot of billable hours here but a very loyal client with whom Roy had a special relationship." Ben said, handing the client's file to Elena which she began flipping through.

"Gray Williams? Are you kidding me? He won a Pulitzer for his first novel, a war story I seem to remember. Since then he's stayed near the top of the New York Times Best Seller list for the last decade, cranking out an average of one novel a year. I'm ashamed to admit that I've never read any of his stuff; I'm not that big on books about war, but wow! I had no idea he was one of the firm's clients."

"You might want to stop by the book store on your way home. He really only wrote one war story. I've read everything he's done. He's a talented author; his power rivals some of the greatest writers of the twentieth century. His stories have always had a painful loneliness to them but somehow, in the end, leave the reader with a sense of hope. I mean, you cry, but the tears are decidedly optimistic as you watch his characters deal with pain and hardship and never give up when you sense that giving up would be easier."

Ben continued. "Elena, Gray Williams is a bit of a recluse. He was badly burned in a helicopter accident during the war. He escaped, unharmed, then went back and pulled everyone else on board to safety. While doing so he received near fatal and horribly disfiguring injuries from the intense fire. He was awarded the Medal of Honor. I understand from an article I read many years ago in the New Yorker, and from a chat Roy and I had, that he went through a long and painful series of surgeries, finally deciding that enough was enough. Roy said that the abject freakishness that burn patients suffer had been corrected but that one side of his face was badly scarred.

I guess he just got tired of being stared at or asked about it over and over in interviews and dropped out of public life. He currently lives alone on a farm somewhere in upstate New York. He and Roy talked often but again, there was a real friendship---a special something between them. He would never talk to anyone else in the firm. Correspondence has been exchanged over the years it's all there in the file. Drop him a line as soon as you can to bring him up to date. You've always had a special relationship with Roy; maybe sharing a piece of that with Mr. Williams will help make you a more palatable substitute."

Ben said good night and Elena continued to peruse the file. Upstate New York and a RFD address. To her surprise she recognized the general location. It couldn't be more than twenty or thirty miles from where she had grown up. In her initial effort to get a handle on who exactly this man was, she did a quick search of the new news data base that the firm had recently procured at significant expense.

There it was in the caption of an old picture of a group of men, heavily bandaged posing in a military hospital ward, and the survivors of the helicopter crash. Matthew

Robert, age nineteen, had been the crew chief and the last survivor pulled from the crash. It had been in the effort to save him that Gray Williams had suffered the majority of his injuries. The picture, included in the article about the first novel did not include their savior, only a caption surmising that this incident had more or less spurred Gray Williams to become a writer. None of those shown in the picture had been willing to be interviewed.

Matthew Roberts could be Roy's grandson or nephew? It had to be. Elena gathered up some papers to include the new client file and headed for her car intent on making two stops on the way home. First, she would swing by the hospital, something she had avoided doing for over a week. Then she would stop at the book store.

Roy didn't recognize Elena but his wife of forty years was very gracious and thanked Elena for coming to visit her husband.

"I owe Roy an awful lot, more than I can ever repay him. He's been a very special friend."

"He loves you like a daughter, Elena. He knew from the first day he met you that you would do great things."

As an afterthought, Elena inquired about the Robert family. "Ruth, I'm going to be handling some of Roy's cases while he's in the hospital. One in particular intrigues me. It a client named Gray Williams, the writer. I pulled up an old news photo of soldiers in a helicopter crash and..."

"Matthew Robert is our grandson. If you'd like to meet him, he and his wife are flying in from the West Coast sometime in the next few weeks. He's an aeronautical engineer and I know he'd love to meet you."

"Ruth, have you ever met Gray Williams?"

"Oh heavens yes! He and Roy were, are, very close and have been since right after the accident. Our only son, Matthew's father, died in a commercial aircraft accident shortly after Matthew returned from the war. I guess in a sense, Roy and I kind of adopted Gray. Even though he is closer to Matthew's age---he was a Captain and the aircraft commander---he became almost like a son to us. He was here a couple of days ago."

"He was here? I thought he was very reclusive."

"As far as public appearances are concerned he is very much so. His parents are deceased and his circle of contacts is very small. He has a brother who lives in Alabama and he is very close to his nieces and nephews. He stays in close personal contact with the other survivors of the crash and fire. He lives on several hundred acres in a remote rural area in New York State in a huge, rambling old log cabin.

On the anniversary of the crash he invites those he is closest to up for a long weekend. He is a very warm and sensitive man, at least as far as those he cares for. A couple of times a year he comes down to the city to visit. He's painfully private. It's strange. His facial disfigurement has faded somewhat with the years and he wears a full beard. You know the second you look at him that he's been the victim of third degree facial burns but I guess when you know the man as well as we know him, you just don't see or think about his scars. I worry much more about the scars on the inside."

"Why say so, Ruth?"

"Have you read any of his books?"

"I'm ashamed to say I haven't."

"You should but you need to start at the beginning and read them in order. Gray is in his middle thirties now. I don't like his current work even though the critics maintain that it his is best. He's getting darker; the hope and commitment to survival that has been the hallmark of his protagonists is ebbing. I also saw it when he was here. I'm not sure that living alone up there in the woods is good for him."

"Did he ever get marry?"

"No, sadly, he never did. He was engaged before he went off to war but she couldn't deal with his injuries. He was psychologically very distant when he came home. We all thought that he had worked through that. I'm pretty sure that he hasn't even dated anyone since he came back. He's still sensitive about his injuries his disfigurement but it goes deeper than the surface. It's as if he feels that he is damaged goods and somehow unworthy of a woman's love. I've seen pictures of him prior to the accident. He was very handsome. He's so damned normal, warm and fun when we all get together. This year, three months before Roy's stroke, I thought he was more withdrawn, that he was turning back to the hopelessness that plagued him through those months in the hospital. It was his writing that saved him; now I fear that something, maybe even his writing is pulling him back into abyss. I worry, we all do."

Elena left the hospital, stopping at the bookstore within a couple of miles of her home. She heeded to Ruth's advice, purchasing the entire anthology of Gray Williams novels. Returning home she was greeted warmly by her two best friends in the world, her pups. After microwaving a prepared entrée for dinner, she poured herself a glass of red wine and began to read through the first Gray Williams novel, the war story that had won him a Pulitzer, as her pups slept at her feet. By sunrise she was a third of the way through the novelist's body of work and starting on her third box of tissues. She was hooked.

She felt as if she had cheated herself by not reading this man's incredible story earlier in life. She took several cat naps as her eyes began to blur from reading. By late Sunday night she had read them all and it had shaken her as no other experience in her life ever had. As she closed the last, the most recent, her body uncontrollably racked with sobs as she recognized that what Roy's wife had told her was painfully evident.

Gray Williams hope and hopefulness was waning. This last, this tenth, magnificent but terribly sad work would quite possibly be the last Gray Williams novel the world would ever experience. And she felt pathetically inadequate to do anything about it. But she had to try.

Email hadn't been perfected yet. The first personal computers were in their infancy and too expensive for most people, not to mention terribly unreliable. The Internet was in its infancy and not available to the general public. Overnight delivery, thanks to FedEX, was in its early days.

CHAPTER THREE

Early Monday morning she began to write a letter to her newest client, one that would not be typed on the office word processor but one that would be received by Gray Williams in her original hand. She had her secretary call FedEX to find out if they even delivered to the remote area in question. They did; in fact, Gray had an account with the company which he frequently used to communicate with his editor and publisher.

This was not the typical letter between an attorney and her client. She shared her special relationship with and love for Roy Robert. She rambled at times. She told of her weekend marathon reading of the author's work. She shared in general terms those times in her life when she had felt inadequate and even hopeless. She spoke of her pups and gave glimpses into her personal life. She then signed it, E.A. Adams, Esq., adding a PS: Please call me so that we can talk about our firm meeting your legal needs.

As she watched the handsome young deliveryman leave her office with the red, white and blue cardboard envelop, she felt completely inadequate and feared that her note to Gray Williams was pitiful.

She had hoped for a phone call. Two days later what she received was a FedEx envelop with a single page, hand written by Warren Davis. It was in its first few sentences almost formal. Then again, this man couldn't even write a one page note to his lawyer without the brilliance of his writing shining through. By the end of the page she saw the hints of warmth that Ruth Robert had stated. She went through the client file for a phone number; there wasn't one. His number was unlisted and he had not volunteered it. He had given no indication of if or when he would next visit the District, let alone whether he had any interest in meeting her.

Two days later, her secretary told her that she had a call waiting from Mr. Williams."This is Elena." She said haltingly into her office phone."Elena? Ah, nice.

That's a very pretty name. I called to thank you for your kind letter; it meant a great deal to me. Ruth spoke very highly of you and told me that you and Roy are very close. It's nice to have one of Roy's friends handling my, ah, what's the word, account? Elena, ah, Ms. Adams l,""Elena will be just fine, Mr. Williams; Adams is my married name, my former husband's name, in fact and..."Well this is a good start, Elena; I'm Gray Williams, my friends call me Gray. Any friend of Roy and Ruth is a friend of mine.

"The two chatted for a few minutes somewhat aimlessly and superficially."Is there any chance we could meet next time you get to the city?" Elena asked, hopefully. There was a very long pause; for a moment she thought they had lost the connection."Elena, I think we both have to face the reality that Roy is not going to come back to us. That knowledge makes it almost unbearably painful for me to see him lying there like that.

I would not think I would make another trip to the city until he passes on. If

I came down before that I would have to visit him and I can't deal with that right now."Elena started to speak. "Gray...""Elena it's been nice getting to chat with you. I need to get to work now but feel free to call anytime. Let me give you my number. I don't answer the phone, I let the machine do that but as soon as I know it's a friend calling, I'll call back. Take care now."

And Gray Williams was gone. Feeling more inadequate than she had in years, she dashed off a quick note on personal stationary and sent it out in the mail. Over the ensuing weeks and months, Roy's health deteriorated. It would soon be time for the family to make a difficult decision as Roy's body was not able to continue without mechanical assistance.

The correspondence between Elena and Gray continued over the next few months; they exchanged short notes every few days. They spoke on the phone at least weekly. Elena wanted desperately to believe that by reaching out to this tortured, lonely man she was providing him some degree of comfort. Initially, his responses became decidedly more upbeat and even jocular at times.

She had sensed his depression coming back and intensifying over the past few weeks. He often did not return her calls or only called her after she had left several messages and then only after a day or two had passed. His letters became less frequent and decidedly darker.

The desperation she felt spurred her to climb well outside of her safety net and execute a bold course of action. She had heard nothing from him in over a week and it scared her. It had required a change of flights to a small commuter job to even get within fifty miles of where Gray lived. She had found a map in the client file, hand drawn by Roy years earlier.

Ruth had confirmed that it was still valid. So here she was, wishing the rental agency had been able to provide a four wheel drive vehicle, creeping along a snowy two lane road in a blinding snow storm. She had driven these roads many years before but nothing still looked familiar. Coming around a sharp curve she felt the skid begin just as she saw the bright lights of the tractor trailer fill her windshield. It was a head on with the truck or the ditch; she chose the latter. It was more than a ditch; it was a steep incline and she came to rest nearly fifty feet below the roadway dazed from the impact, scared out of her mind and terribly unsure as to what the future held for her.

There was a car in the ditch. He only saw it after he passed. He touched the pistol jammed between the seats at his side; it was the one he had carried into war so many years before. It was also the one that would soon end his torment, but not yet.

There was someone in trouble, maybe injured and they should not suffer due to his weakness. It was time to do what he had to do, he thought to himself grimly save someone in need. For him it was too late for salvation. This won't take long, he mused; death can wait, certainly my own death.

Turning on his flashers, he cautiously backed up to confirm his suspicions. He jumped down from the massive, old Ram truck. It wasn't one of the new pretty ones, but the old kind that fireman and forest rangers used. It would literally drive over small trees or through fences if needed and climb the steepest grade.

As the snow continued to fall in what would become the worst blizzard in over fifty years, he was glad he owned it. He pulled as far off the road as possible, grabbed a hand full of flares and ran a hundred yards or so in each direction to mark the accident. He doubted that anyone would be coming along.

While this was a US highway, it was only two lanes and there were faster four lane routes that would get you to the same place. Most of the traffic was locals; most locals weren't dumb enough to be out in this stuff.

He was returning from a neighbor's farm having helped him move a herd into his barn. As he approached the car, he saw that it was a late model rental. The rear lights were blinking faintly and the engine was not running. He hoped everyone was unhurt.

The hospital was over an hour away and it was doubtful that an ambulance could get there quickly; the few available were up to their butts in weather related issues.

No skis perched on a roof rack; the nearest ski resort was some distance away but it was very doubtful that the car's occupants would choose this route if skiing was in their plans; sometimes they got lost. He banged on the window.

He couldn't really see through the fogged windows. With its dying breath, the battery managed to provide enough juice to roll the window down a little more than half way. He was startled to come face to face with a disheveled, but still very attractive blond women. She looked scared, cold, wet and disoriented. "Are you okay?" He asked softly, trying to smile enough to calm her fears, but not so much that he looked like a potential rapist.

Elena was very cold, wet and miserable. She should never have set out on this trek, she thought to herself, knowing that the weather forecast was ugly. But she was on a mission, wasn't she? A mission to save someone even thought she had no idea what she was going to say or do when she got there. She had no idea exactly where she was in relation to Gray Williams' log cabin. She had tried to start the car, but it wouldn't start. When she had gotten out surveying the damage, she instantly realized that she could never have driven the car back up the steep embankment.

For too long she had fruitlessly stood out in the driving snow at the road's edge, hoping for a passing car. None came. She had slid and tumbled back down to her rental car soaked and on the verge of frostbite.

She decided she would have a better chance of surviving in the car. With no heat and the rapidly deepening snow, she had begun to believe that she might not get out of this one. She had just been drifting off into what most probably would have been that long sleep that ultimately becomes permanent.

The tap on the window jolt her up."Are you okay?" He repeated, a little louder this time. "Hi! Let's get you out of there and up in the truck where it's a little warmer."He opened the door and helped her out of the car and up the embankment.

At some point she was sure she mumbled her name."I don't know what would have happened if you hadn't come along. Thank you." she whispered. He almost lifted her into the passenger side of the huge truck, no small feat considering she was a bit over five foot ten inches. He seemed to do so as if she was a feather pillow."Stay here in the truck and get warm. There's reasonable coffee in the thermos. I'm sorry that there's nothing to eat. I'm going to go take a look at your car." He said, and slammed the solid door shut. She wasn't sure she would even recognize him when he returned. He was a tall man, certainly over six feet.

She had caught his smile in spite of his beard and the heavy scarf wrapped around his face to protect against the driving snow. He was not fat. He was wearing a heavy parka, jeans and some sort of boots, brown she recalled. How old was he? He was not her junior by much but nor did he have the carriage of an older man. As she took in her surroundings in the massive truck cab, she quickly realized he didn't smoke.

CHAPTER FOUR

The cab was spotless; there was a bible and another book on the center tray. There was a worn, leather bound book of Shakespeare's Sonnets. There was music playing, she assumed from the tape player. It was Mozart; it was one of her favorites, one of the Concertos, but she couldn't remember which one. There was a gun rack behind her; it contained a shot gun and a hunting rifle. She had grown up with guns and didn't fear them.

There was food after all. She opened the glove compartment and found an aged power bar and a silver flask. Fortunately, the power bar was foil wrapped and not spoiled. She thought, what the hell, and took a big swig from the silver flask. It was brandy; it was pretty good brandy. She had another swig and, not wanting to be greedy, returned the flask to its rightful place. Who the hell is this guy?

Meanwhile, he had popped the hood on the rental and determined that there was little he could do, particularly in the middle of a blizzard. He suspected that she had cracked the distributor cap; he knew he didn't have any distributor caps back at the house. He decided it made sense to get the thing out of the ditch and try to tow in out of the right of way. He surveyed the terrain and came up with a plan. He returned to the truck, pleased to note that his passenger, while still cold and disheveled, seemed to be recovering.

"That sucker is not going to start. Something broke when you tumbled over the embankment, probably the distributor cap. I'm going to pull it out of the ditch and tow it down the road to someplace where it will be safe." He said, putting the truck in gear and beginning to maneuver to recover her rental car.

He skillfully moved the truck into position; he hopped out of the truck and began unwinding the winch that this kind of truck comes with from the factory. He ran down the embankment and hooked the winch under the rear axle. Returning to the front of the truck, he engaged the winch.

The car began its slow climb back to the edge of the roadway. He then disconnected the winch and, repositioning the truck, hooked a tow bar to the front bumper.

He climbed back up in the cab. "This isn't a tow truck so I can't get the drive wheels off the ground. Normally towing like this isn't very good for the transmission, but we don't have far to go, and hell, it is a rental." He informed her.

About a mile down the road, he pulled off to the entrance of an old barn. He jumped out of the truck, opened the barn door and backed the towed vehicle skillfully inside. Popping the trunk, he recovered her suitcase and threw it behind the front seat.

"When the blizzard's over, we can probably get old Mark Thompson out of that little town you passed about fifteen miles back to come out here and fix it; I doubt that the rental company will be able to get to it for several days." He quietly informed her.

He drove around behind the barn and started up a very steep gravel road. Elena felt the raw power as the truck surged up the mountain road through snow that was now already over a foot deep. The old Ram never faltered.

They arrived a few minutes later at the top of a small mountain, she assumed; the snow was coming down so hard that she wasn't absolutely sure. To her right was an open horse barn; she noticed two horses huddled together near the back of the structure.

There were other buildings including another barn but she couldn't really pick out detail. The house was set just below the top of the mountain; it was a large, rustic log cabin with a broad front porch, not uncommon in this part of the country. He pulled the truck under a car port that was attached to the house.

He jumped out and came around to help her down and recovered her suitcase. They entered the house through the kitchen, which was large, spacious and well appointed. They were quickly greeted by two dogs, one sled dog ancestry and a big black Lab. This was a man's house she thought to herself; there was no hint of feminine frilliness."The guest bedroom and bathroom is at the top of the stairs on the left. Make yourself comfortable. I'll get something going on the stove to get you warmed up.

There are some sweats that I inadvertently shrunk in the dryer in the closet in there and I'm sure you can find something that will fit if you didn't bring a warm change of clothes. Bring your wet clothes down when you're done and we'll throw them in the washer." He said, over his shoulder. She thanked him and, taking her suitcase, headed up the stairs. The warm water was soon caressing her naked body and bringing her back to life.

Realizing as she exited the shower that nothing she had so hurriedly packed fit the bill, she went with a pair of fleece sweats she dug out of the linen closet. Descending the stairs, she was grateful that her benefactor had stoked the massive stone fireplace; the fire was a roaring and inviting one.

Who was this man? She had no doubt that he had probably saved her life. She hadn't really seen his face and they had not had a chance to introduce themselves. As she heard the bustle from the kitchen she perused the book shelves on either side of the grand fireplace. His books were obviously for reading not for show. The selection was eclectic, even academic in its diversity. She chuckled at the fact that the shelves were devoid of popular current fiction. No Gray Williams volumes were in evidence.

CHAPTER FIVE

And then she saw it. A picture, prominently displayed, almost enshrined above the fireplace. She knew that picture. She had once owned the exact same pose but it had been lost, much to her regret, during one of her many moves over the years. It was a picture of her. She was smiling. She had on a long white prom dress and an orchid corsage. There was a handsome young man standing next to her wearing a tux, grasping her hand, gazing into her eyes.

She grabbed the picture off the shelf and clutched it to her breast. She inhaled sharply and then gasped. The gasp became a sob. She could not hold back the ensuing flood of tears as she gripped that special picture. She heard her host placing plates on the table just outside the kitchen. Spinning around, she spoke. Her voice cracked as she uttered a single word, more of a question than a statement.

"Dustin?"

He froze. His head still turned away from her, as if he could not look at her.

"I seem to recall once going by that name." He said, his body still turned away.

She ran toward him, placing the framed photo on the table between them. "Justine? Don't you recognize me, oh hell, why should you. It's been seventeen years. That's you standing next to me in that picture, isn't it? That's us on what was for me the most magical night of my life." She said, moving close to him, taking his hand, touching his face and gently turning it toward her own.

"Elena?" He whispered.

And as Elena saw the deep scars still visible under his full beard; her confusion was instantly replaced by complete recognition. It all fell into place. As he vainly tried to resist, she would have none of it. Taking his arms she placed them around her. Cupping his face in her hands she kissed him. And it was with that kiss, a kiss as magical as the first time a boy, this boy, had ever kissed her so many years ago;

Elena brought Gray Williams, born Dustin Warner, back from the edge of the abyss. He stopped fighting her and took her in his arms as he had that special night.

"Don't fight me Dustin, not now, not ever again. I won't let you slip away twice in the same life time."

"Never Elena, Never.

 I won't leave you. Thank you.

Thank you for coming back to me.

Saving me"

.....

And then he started to babble almost incoherently as he realized that he really only knew one special woman name Elena. The one who had touched his heart indelibly at their senior prom was the same Elena who had been desperately trying to pull him back from the edge over the last several months. She had come closer to failing than she could have known. She had risked everything including her own life to come back for him, to pull him from that burning crash site which his life had become. Elena silenced him with her lips and held him as tightly as he had held her on her parents' door step.

Many don't believe in the healing power of another's touch; it's easy to deride faith healers as little more than con artists. But in those few moments, as Dustin and Maryanne stood together, wrapped in each other's arms with their lips pressed tightly together and their tears intermingling, their two hearts connected again as they had connected so many years before.

As each heart broke free and accepted the other, all of the hurt, all of the regret, all of the pain, all of the heartache and all of the disappointment both had held on to for far too long was swept away as if a wave of holy water had washed over them.

Dustin's once hopeful and optimistic spirit returned in the arms of the special girl who had captured his heart those many years before. The cynical book reviewers were almost disappointed as his work became much brighter and even more uplifting. His loyal readers, on the other hand, were relieved, for they too had thought that they were close to losing him.

Dustin and Elena wept softly together as their dear friend Roy was laid to rest a few weeks later; it saddened them both that the dear old man had not been there to be part of their happiness together.

Elena never became a federal judge in spite of several attempts to entice her in that direction. She retired from the law, changing her last name one final time. Gray Williams became Dustin Warner again, venturing boldly out in public when the need arose.

They spent many special days alone together on that enigmatic mountain farm in New York, for both were, at heart, very private people. It was the place in which Dustin had almost been lost but also the place in which two very special, nice, sweet, caring and deserving people found each other and found enduring love.

As the years went on their solitude was delightfully broken by the voices of young children. No matter where they resided together, they always found time in the year to return to that old log cabin where their life together had almost ended before it began. THE END